About the Book

Robbie Cameron stood at the edge of Hidden Hollow and looked down on the thick, gnarled oaks and dark pines that surrounded the old Duncan place. A faint mist hung over the battered barn and the moonlight threw an eerie glow around the ragged fence. It gave the dark, neglected buildings an enchanted, unreal look.

Robbie wished that Daisy hadn't picked Halloween Night to run away and that her hoofprints didn't lead into Hidden Hollow. But he had to find Daisy.

What happens to Robbie and how he makes some very special friends is a Halloween adventure that all children will love.

Highland Halloween

by Wilma Pitchford Hays

illustrated by Peter Burchard

Coward-McCann, Inc. New York

80120

To Alice

Prologue

Halloween came to us from old folk customs of the Celts. The Celts were people who lived in the British Isles long ago; Scottish Highlanders, Welsh, Britons and some of the Irish. Their customs have changed a great deal since the earliest festivals.

Long ago people often worshiped several gods. Among the Celtic gods were the Sun God and his opposite, Samhain, Lord of the Dead and Prince of Darkness.

The Celts, led by their Druid priests, celebrated a joint festival in honor of these two gods. They thanked the Sun God for the harvest, and they performed mysterious rites to strengthen the Sun God during the six months of winter when he lost his power (light).

They believed that during the winter Samhain was in power. They honored him on the first day of November to please him and keep him from doing them any harm. They believed that Samhain called spirits to walk the earth on the night before the day set to honor him.

On the eve of Samhain Day, the Celts lighted bonfires to welcome winter, but also to frighten off the evil spirits. They thought that witches and ghosts were afraid of light and would not come near an open fire.

Many years later, after the Celts accepted the one God, the Church changed the pagan festival of Samhain to a day on which to honor *all* saints. The Church called it Allhallows or Hallowmas, a solemn day. But the old customs still cling to the night *before* All Saints' Day, the night called Halloween.

Although the customs have changed greatly, we can still see traces of these long-ago times in the things we do on Halloween. We still like to shiver at the thought of witches and ghosts abroad that night, although we no longer believe in them.

Our idea of Jack-o'-lantern may have come from the Celt custom of carrying a light to ward off spirits if people had to leave their homes on Samhain Eve. They hollowed out large turnips in which to carry their lights to keep the wind from blowing them out. Sometimes the people wore masks and costumes so the spirits could not recognize them.

Cats were sacred to the Druid Celts. They believed that black cats, in particular, were friends of witches and could bring storms. A black cat might even be an evil spirit in disguise. Often in those days a black cat on a silver chain was left to guard treasures, for no one would pass by a black cat.

Perhaps our "trick or treat" is distantly related to an old custom which came after the church changed Samhain Day to All Saints' Day. Boys called "soulers" used to walk the streets singing and begging, "A soule-cake, a soule-cake, have mercy on all Christian soules — for a soule-cake!" People from the houses would give the boys square baked buns dotted with currants.

In the highlands of Scotland the children used to hunt sticks and leaves for Halloween fires. Families gathered about these fires to sing, play games, and dance to the music of bagpipes. They brought nuts and apples to eat.

Later, during the pioneer days, Scottish Highlanders came to America to live. The rivers and peaks and hollows (valleys) of the Great Smoky Mountains reminded them of their homes in Scotland. They loved the beauty and wild freedom of the southern mountains and settled there. Although their children's children have been loyal Americans for years, many of them still know the ways of their Highland ancestors.

*   *   *

HIGHLAND HALLOWEEN

"So-o-o, Boss! So-o-o, Bossy," Robbie Cameron called as he hunted for Daisy-cow on a slope of the Great Smoky Mountains.

Daisy knew when it was milking time, Robbie thought. Usually she came to meet him, switching her tail to drive the flies from her brindled sides. And when he called to her, she lifted her short-horned head and lowed in answer, "Mo-ooo."

But this evening Daisy was nowhere to be found. She was not in her pasture in Lonesome Hollow. Not among the gnarled oaks beyond. Not under the dark pines farther up the mountain.

She must have run away during the storm this afternoon. Daisy had never liked rain and thunder and lightning. How much farther had she gone?

Robbie came on Daisy's hoofprints at the edge of a steep slope. He stopped and looked down. In the narrow hollow below, the Little Fear River was running over its banks. A waterfall, usually only a tinkling trickle, was now a foaming, roaring torrent.

Robbie shaded his gray eyes with his hand. He looked hard for a brindled cow among the yellow and brown leaves of the trees along the river. He saw a movement in a green thicket. It might be Daisy, but it could be a deer or a black bear.

He called again, "So-o-o, Bossy!"

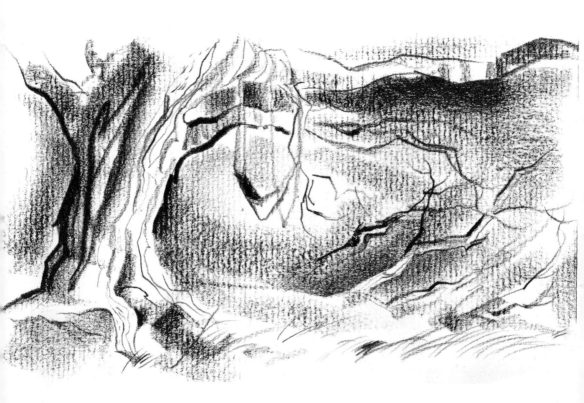

His voice echoed in the hollow, "Boss-eee-eee-eee."

It gave Robbie a queer feeling as if a ghost answered him. Not that he really believed in ghosts. Still, he wished that Daisy had not picked Halloween night to run away, and that her hoofprints did not lead into Hidden Hollow.

Robbie had never entered Hidden Hollow even in the daytime. He and his friend, Archie Blake, had fished right up to the waterfall at the end of the hollow, but never above it.

For there, beside the river where the great oaks were thickest, was an old house where something terrible had happened a long time ago. In the days when mountain men used to end bitter quarrels with shotguns, three Duncan men had been shot here. Granny Duncan had lost her husband and her two sons at dusk, as they came from the barn with milk pails in their hands.

Granny Duncan had been a young woman then. She had kept on living in the house alone. She let it be known that anyone who ever came on her land would wish he hadn't. That was forty years ago but people were still a little afraid of Hidden Hollow and Granny Duncan.

Robbie ran his hand through his dark red hair and looked at Daisy's hoofprints. The prints were deep on the muddy slope, then they disappeared in a thick yellow carpet of fallen leaves.

Robbie heard a rustle behind him. He

jumped and felt a little foolish when he saw only a squirrel scurrying past. Then he heard a moan and a groan. His heart beat fast until the moan turned into a snicker.

Robbie called, "You, Archie Blake, come out."

Archie stepped from behind a tree, brushing moss from his dark hair and grinning. Archie was never happier than when he was playing jokes on people, although he was frightened easily enough himself.

"Did you think I was one of the Duncan ghosts?" Archie teased. "Don't worry—everyone says those ghosts stay near the barn."

Robbie didn't think Archie was very funny, not with the sun dropping behind the peaks of the hogback, and Halloween night coming on.

"How did you know where to find me?" he asked.

"Your mother wanted me to bring you your supper," Archie said, handing Robbie a paper sack. "She had to take your sisters to the Halloween party and you weren't home yet. I heard you calling the cow—and found you."

"Thanks, I am hungry," Robbie said. He bit into a sandwich and pointed to Daisy's hoofprints leading into Hidden Hollow.

Archie whistled. "We can't go down there. It'll soon be dark."

"I have to," Robbie said. "She's the only cow we have. If she fell in the river or stepped in a spring hole, what would we do for milk? Besides, I wouldn't want anything to happen to Daisy."

"If we don't go back before dark," Archie said, "we could get lost in these woods and miss the Halloween bonfire and the fun."

"I want to go to the party," Robbie said, "but I have to find Daisy first."

He stepped on a boulder where he could see better into the hollow. Archie climbed up and stood beside him.

They could see a footbridge of logs almost covered by muddy floodwater. Beyond the river was a ragged fence around a log cabin in a wilderness of weeds and briers. Robbie could see a battered barn which leaned as if it was about to fall down. It made his neck prickle to look at the huddle of neglected buildings. No wonder people said the Duncan place was haunted.

He saw an old woman come from the cabin
and hang sheets on a clothesline.

"A queer time to be hanging out sheets,"
Archie said.

"Maybe she couldn't get them dry today be-
cause of the storm," Robbie said.

"Doesn't she look just like a witch?" Archie
asked.

Granny Duncan's old-fashioned dark skirts
billowed in the wind. Her long white hair blew

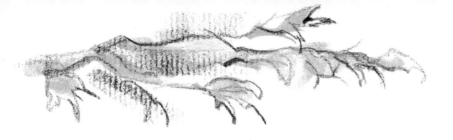

across her face. Robbie had to admit that she looked like someone he wouldn't want to meet on a dark night. But he couldn't help feeling sorry for her. It must be hard to live alone in that wreck of a house with its tottering chim-

ney. She was too old to keep the house in repair or the weeds cut.

"Well, we aren't going to find Daisy, standing here," Robbie said. "Are you coming with me?"

"A choice between the devil and the deep blue sea!" Archie said. "If I go back, I must go through the dark woods alone — I guess I'll go with you."

Robbie laughed and led the way down the slope. "So-o-o, Bossy," he called.

It was easy walking for a short distance while the bright yellow leaves lighted the hillside. Then the boys came upon ground that was spongy. They had to move fast to keep from sinking into a spring hole. Robbie pushed his way through a tangle of grapevines, and heard a crash. He turned and found Archie sprawled on the ground.

"Ouch," Archie cried, rubbing his ankle.

Robbie waited and saw that his friend was

limping when he tried to walk. He helped Archie to a hummock of grass in the open center of the thicket. "Does it hurt much?" he asked.

Archie stooped and felt his ankle, which showed a long scratch. "I guess I'll live," he said. "That is, if we find our way out of here. It's sure getting dark fast."

Robbie looked at the tangle of trees around them. He hoped to see a broken branch to show which way Daisy might have gone. In the stillness, he felt suddenly that something was watching him. He knew that Archie felt it, too. For once, his friend was very quiet, listening.

Robbie couldn't say that he heard anything. Yet he *knew* there was something behind him. Slowly he turned his head.

From the thicket close to the ground, two unblinking yellow eyes stared at him. They belonged to the blackest cat that Robbie had ever seen. Its back was arched, every hair bristling. Its long tail twitched as it watched the boys.

"A black cat," Archie whispered. "Granny Duncan's a witch for sure! Let's get out of here."

"Wait," Robbie said. His heart was thumping but he had seen something behind the black cat. Peering from the thicket was a boy about his own age. He had an impish face, deeply tanned beneath a tangle of hair as dark red as Robbie's own.

"Hello," Robbie managed to say. "What are you doing here?"

"*I* live here," the boy said. "What are *you* doing on Duncan land?"

Archie caught Robbie's elbow. "Look," he said in a low voice. "He has a dog with him that looks like a wolf, if a wolf was brown. Don't say anything to make him mad at us."

The hair of the wolf-dog bristled. The black cat spit. The boy with the impish face stepped from the thicket. He wore a ragged blue shirt and jeans held up by a worn leather strap over one shoulder. His bare legs and feet were as brown as if he had always lived outdoors.

He scowled. "I ken why you're here — to play Halloween tricks on Granny Duncan."

"Oh, no," Robbie cried. "We came hunting my lost cow, Daisy. The storm scared her and she ran away."

"I didna see a cow," the boy said. "I didna hear a cow."

"She came into the hollow," Robbie said.

"I'm afraid she will get hurt if we don't find her."

The boy nodded, more friendly now. "Aye, it's rough country here," he said. "I'll help you find her."

"Thank you," Robbie said. "My name is Robbie Cameron and my friend is Archie Blake."

"I'm Malcolm Duncan," the boy said. "I've come from the other side of the hogback to live with Granny Duncan. She wouldn't leave her home and she couldn't be left alone any longer, so I was sent."

"Sent?" Robbie asked.

"By the family, of course," Malcolm answered. "We all gathered in a meeting and decided. I can best be spared and I'm strong." He held out a sturdy brown arm and flexed his muscles. "I can look after her."

Robbie knew that many of the old Scottish clan customs were still observed in the mountain country. One of the strongest customs was that a family looked after their own old relatives. He had heard that some of Granny's kin came each month from the other side of the mountain to bring supplies to her.

"You're her grandson?" he asked.

"Her grandnephew," Malcolm said.

Archie had not said a word, which was so unlike him that Robbie turned to see what was the matter. Archie was watching the strange boy as if he wasn't sure that Malcolm was real.

"We'd better look for Daisy," Robbie said.

"Maybe your cow was bewitched," Malcolm said. "Dinna remember it was Halloween, and tie a knot on her tail to keep evil spirits away?"

Robbie saw Malcolm's grin and knew that he was joking, but Archie looked alarmed.

"I think we'd better go different ways to hunt the cow," Archie said.

"I'll go this way," Malcolm said, pointing, "and you go that way. The cow would naturally go downhill toward the river. It's easier walking. We'll meet at the footbridge. If you

get lost, holler. I'll find you. I know my way
even in the dark."

He disappeared into the thicket followed by
the wolf-dog and the black cat.

"Holler nothing!" Archie whispered as soon
as Malcolm was gone. "I hope we never see
that boy again. Don't you know who he is?"

Robbie shook his head.

"The midnight boy," Archie said. "Remember, Old Lon described him to us."

Of course, Robbie remembered now. Old

Lon Allen, who liked to fish at night, claimed he had seen a wild boy and a wolf walking in the woods on moonlight nights. And when Lon called to him, the boy faded away into the mist. "That midnight boy just plumb vanished," Old Lon had told the boys, "like a puff of smoke."

"You know Old Lon likes to tell tall tales," Robbie said now to Archie. "No one believes him."

"*This* time Old Lon was telling the truth,"

Archie said. "Wild boy, wolf-dog, black cat and all! I'm getting out of here."

"Old Lon just didn't know *who* Malcolm was," Robbie insisted. "He's not wild. You saw him yourself and he offered to help us. Come on."

Darkness had fallen now. There was barely enough light to keep them from bumping into the dark trunks of trees.

As the boys moved toward the river, Robbie began calling the cow again. For the life of him, he couldn't sing out loud and strong, as he had in the daylight. He kept up a low "So-o-o, Bossy," and hoped he would hear Daisy low in answer.

By the time the boys reached the river, the moon had risen and gave more light. A faint mist hung over the house and the leaning barn across the water. It gave the dark neglected buildings an enchanted unreal look.

Robbie stopped at the narrow footbridge of logs. The flood was so high that the center of

the sagging bridge had sunk under the dark water. He saw that both ends of the bridge were firm. It could be crossed, but he had no wish to go nearer the Duncan place.

"We'd better wait here for Malcolm," he said.

"How I wish I was at the bonfire party at the school," Archie said. He stopped and looked at Robbie. "I just thought — what if Granny Duncan's boy tries to come to school?"

Robbie knew what Archie was thinking. No boy or girl would welcome the stranger from Hidden Hollow. They would all be careful about playing with someone from the Duncan house.

"Maybe if we were his friends," Robbie began.

"Not me," Archie said. "If I ever get out of here, I'll never have anything to do with Hidden Hollow again."

Rustling noises in the bushes nearby startled the boys into silence. Robbie looked at the

mist, like the thinnest of white veils over everything in the hollow, and he couldn't help
agreeing with Archie. But how could they get
out of this strange place and find their way
home?

From the woods directly behind them came
a hair-raising cry. The boys leaped forward.
They were halfway across the footbridge before the cry came again and they knew what it
was. With the cold floodwater swirling about
their ankles, they stopped in the middle of the
narrow bridge.

"Only a hoot owl," Robbie said shakily.

But Archie, who was ahead, pointed a wav-
ering finger at the leaning barn. "Look," he
whispered. "The Duncan ghost, coming
around the corner."

Through the pale mist, Robbie saw a large
white shape moving. He didn't believe in
ghosts but he couldn't doubt his own eyes. The
white shrouded figure was coming directly
toward the bridge as if it had heard his voice.

"Run," Archie cried.

Robbie couldn't move. Archie pushed past him and slipped. The boys caught each other and fell forward against the old railing. As the rotten rails of the bridge gave way, the boys fell together into the river.

The force of the cold water closing over their heads broke their hold on each other. In an instant Robbie was swept downstream. He came to the surface, and gasped for breath. He tried to swim but the current was too swift. He was flung against something hard. He caught at it and pulled himself up, sputtering.

He found that he had his arm over the trunk of a tree fallen across the water.

He clung to it. When he could get his breath he shouted, "Archie, where are you?"

"Here," Archie called.

He had caught in the thick branches of the tree. He crawled hand over hand along the swaying tree trunk to Robbie. The cold water had chilled him and his teeth were chattering.

The boys made their way to the end of the trunk where the deep roots of the tree still clung to the earth. They let their feet down,

trying to touch bottom, but the mad water swung their bodies out into the channel. They hugged the tree trunk and looked at each other.

The Duncan shore of the river wasn't more than ten feet away. But it was ten feet of swirling, forceful water. If they tried to swim for it, they could be swept downstream. They could hear the roar of the waterfall as it plunged over the cliff below them.

Then they heard a shout. Malcolm was running across the footbridge. But when he reached the shore, he didn't turn toward the boys. He ran to the Duncan house.

"He's not going to help us," Archie said. "He's Granny Duncan's boy, and she *said* anyone coming on Duncan land would wish he hadn't."

Robbie didn't know what to think. His hands were numb with cold. He couldn't hang on much longer. He didn't know how much longer the tree roots would hold against the swift water. He and Archie had to do something.

"Maybe we better try to swim," he said. "I'll go first, and if I make it —"

He was interrupted by Malcolm calling from the riverbank. "I've got Granny's wool plaid," he shouted. "I've tied a rock into one corner of it. Catch! Here it comes."

Robbie heard the plop of the rock as it hit the water beside him. The boys hadn't gathered their wits in time to catch it. Malcolm was already drawing the heavy plaid back to him.

"Here it comes again," he cried.

Robbie lunged and grabbed for the plaid as it sailed over his head. He missed.

Archie shouted, "I've got it."

Robbie caught hold of the soggy wool, too, and held it tightly. He watched Malcolm brace himself behind a tree at the edge of the water.

"I have the plaid knotted around the tree," Malcolm called. "Come away. It'll hold."

Clinging to the plaid, the two boys reached the shore. They staggered onto the grassy bank. They were choking, half-drowned, and blind and deaf from the water in their eyes and ears. Malcolm came between them and took each boy by an arm.

"You must get dry," he said. "Lucky that Granny has a big fire in the fireplace for our Halloween."

Weak as they were, both boys tried to draw back. "We — we're all right," Robbie said. "Thank you —"

"You're cold as stones," Malcolm said. "You could get pneumonia."

He led them directly to the house. Granny Duncan was holding the door open. Beyond her was the red glow of the fire lighting the room.

Come what may, Robbie thought, it's warm inside. He was so tired he couldn't move another step.

Malcolm took the boys to the cookroom,

which was lighted by kerosene lamps above the washbasin and the wood-burning stove. They took off their wet clothes and wrapped themselves in quilts which Malcolm brought them.

"Now come back to the sitting room," he said. "You'll soon be warm by the fire."

They followed him. Granny Duncan handed them cups of tea. "This will cure your chills," she said.

Robbie sniffed the brew in the cup. He tasted it. It was a little like tea, but more like herbs. Its fragrance reminded him of something he had smelled before. He drank again and then he knew.

It smelled like the spicebush and fern which got in his eyes when he knelt to drink from a spring in the woods. He remembered that old mountain women knew which roots and bark and plants were healing. He drank the tea. It warmed him all through, just as Granny said it would.

Robbie looked more closely at the quilt
wrapped about him. It was made of small
scraps of bright cotton sewed carefully by
hand in overlapping circles on a light back-
ground. It was very like the quilt on his own
bed at home.

Granny Duncan saw him looking at it. " 'Tis

a bonny quilt pattern, the double-wedding-ring," she said. "I've made lots of quilts here alone these many years, patterns of dove-in-the-window and nine-patch, too."

Robbie nodded. "My grandmother and mother are quilting a nine-patch now," he said, "to sell at the fall fair."

"I used to help with the fairs in the town," Granny said, "before—" She stood up quickly. "Na-na. I dinna think, letting my tongue run on so, when you must be hungry.

"Malcolm and I air having a party tonight. The Halloween buns and friedcakes air ready. There's na reason we canna have refreshments to begin the party, instead of to end it."

When the old woman went into the cook-room, Archie whispered to Robbie. "With her hair combed, she doesn't look like a witch, and she surely doesn't act like one, either."

"That's what I was thinking," Robbie said.

Malcolm came in with their wet clothing. "I wrung the water from them," he said.

"They'll dry in an hour beside the fire. You'll get home before your mothers worry too much."

Robbie looked at Archie and Archie looked at Robbie. They had been so glad to be dry and warm again. They had forgotten about the problem of getting out of this strange hollow in the dark.

"Our families are at the bonfire party at the schoolhouse," Robbie said. "They'll be too busy to miss us for a while."

"We'd be at the party, too," Archie said, "if it wasn't for that pesky old Daisy-cow."

Malcolm said, "I'm thankful to Daisy. I mean to start to school on Monday. It will be bonny to have friends."

Archie nudged Robbie. Robbie was about to say that, of course, they would be his friends, when there was a scratching at the door. Malcolm opened it. The wolf-dog and black cat bounded in. Robbie caught a glimpse of the dark leaning barn, and remembered the ghost. He couldn't say a word.

The dog went to the fire and the cat disappeared into the shadows. Granny Duncan returned with a plate of home-baked Halloween buns and golden doughnuts, and a bowl of red apples polished until they shone.

"Aye," she said. " 'Tis a long time since this old house welcomed company. And I did want the lad to have a real old Highland Halloween party. Our family's never forgotten the bonny Highland ways."

Malcolm brought hot cocoa and a jug of sweet apple cider and placed them on the old

table, which looked as if it was hand-hewn from a thick slab of oak.

The boys were warm now. They fastened their quilts under their arms to set their hands free. They pulled their chairs to the table and faced the fire. Everything tasted so good that the refreshments were soon gone.

"Now it's time for the fun," Malcolm said.

"Aye," Granny said. " 'Tis too bad you lads air not dressed to play the pipes and dance to the crossed blades. But you can sing along with Malcolm."

Robbie was glad he didn't have to admit to the old woman that neither he nor Archie, for all their Scottish names, knew how to play the bagpipes or dance over the crossed claymores.

"I'll put on my kilts," Malcolm said and went into a back room.

Granny took the dishes to the cookroom. Robbie looked at the dog, which lay before the fire with its head on its front paws. The dog yawned and closed its eyes again.

"He doesn't look much like a wolf now," Robbie said.

"No, he doesn't," Archie agreed.

The boys heard a soft mewing sound. It seemed to come from behind the woodbox by the fireplace. They went to the woodbox and bent to look. The black cat lay in a nest made of a faded blue shirt. Beside her were two kittens as black as she. She warned the boys away with her yellow eyes and switching tail. The kittens tumbled over each other and meowed. The mother licked them comfortingly in turn.

Archie whistled. "She's proud as peaches of those kittens," he said.

Robbie nodded. "I'm beginning to feel more foolish all the time," he said. "Our witch's black cat has turned out to be only a proud mother. Granny Duncan is an old lady who has been kind to us. Even this house, which we were afraid of, has helped us become warm and dry. It doesn't seem haunted now, does it?"

"No," Archie answered. "But you're forgetting something. We *did* see a ghost. You know we did. It was white and it floated right at us. You can't explain *that* away."

Robbie knew that Archie was right. A shrouded white *something* had come straight toward them through the mist. Both of them had seen it. They had fallen into the river trying to escape it.

Granny Duncan came back into the room. "Here's Malcolm," she said. "You'll never see a bonnier lad. The kilts were my own grandfather's, and the bagpipes were his, too."

The moment Robbie saw Malcolm he knew that the boy wasn't wearing ordinary kilts. He wore "braws," the dress kilts of his clan. He stopped before Granny. He looked tall with his head held high and his long brown bare legs spaced wide.

"You're splendid," Robbie cried.

"Like a picture in a book," Archie said.

Malcolm's kilt and the plaid he wore over his shoulder were red, finely crossed with blue and green. His sporran was of flowing white goat's hair, trimmed with tassels of silver.

"I should be wearing buckled shoes and stockings and red garters," he said, "but they're worn out."

"Fetch down the blades, lad," the old woman said.

Malcolm reached above the mantel for the two claymores hung there. He lifted the heavy two-edged swords and crossed their long blades upon the floor before the fireplace.

"I dinna ken how nimble I'll be," he said, "playing the pipes and dancing at the same time."

"Aye, you should have a piper," Granny Duncan agreed, "but you'll manage, lad. And if I wasn't so old, I'd show you a step or two."

Robbie saw that the old woman's wrinkled hands were keeping time to music that only she seemed to hear. Her dark eyes shone with pride as she watched her grandnephew stalk slowly around the swords, then lift the pipes to play.

The music of the bagpipes began slowly, droning a heartbreaking rhythm that made Robbie swallow. Malcolm leaped in and out among the crossed blades, playing faster and faster. The firelight winked on the silver tassels of his sporran.

The music grew more warlike and Malcolm leaped higher. On and on, faster and faster, went the wild skirl of the music. Finally he bent suddenly forward and left the pipes on the floor. He leaped up, feet braced wide, and thrust the two crossed blades high above his dark red head.

For a long moment no one spoke. The wild dance and wilder music had touched something inside Robbie. They brought back memories he didn't know he had. He blinked rapidly and looked at the old woman. She sat without moving, her long bony fingers clutching her black skirts. Tears rolled down her wrinkled cheeks.

Malcolm's arms dropped to his sides. "Granny," he asked, "dinna I remember it right?"

"Aye," she said as if she were waking from a dream. "Thank ye, lad."

He dropped down beside the dog, who had lain with his ears flattened to his head and watched his master's leaps with anxious eyes.

"I canna do more until I rest. It's your turn. What can you do?" he asked the boys.

"I play a pretty good game of baseball," Archie said, grinning, "but that's about all."

"Will you teach me to play baseball when I come to school?" Malcolm asked. "In the school I went to, we dinna have enough boys for a team."

Robbie looked at Archie and they smiled. There was no doubt in their minds now that they wanted to be Malcolm's friend.

"We will," Robbie said, "and the kids will all want to hear you play the pipes at our next school party."

Granny Duncan told them then of the days

when she was young. Aye, then the Great
Smoky Mountains were really wild. There
were no towns and no stores. Her papa, her
brothers and her uncles took their long-rifles
and hunted and fished wherever they pleased.

"All we had to eat was wild game and corn bread and a little sweetin'," she said. "But we dinna feel poor. We have the bonniest trees and flowers and songbirds in the world right here among these peaks and hollers. And we ken how to be glad in our hearts.

"We had parties around the fireplace, with storytellin' and ballad singin'. Aye, the songs we made up! One would sing a line. Another would add a line to it, whatever came into his mind."

"It's easy to do," Malcolm said. "Dinna ever try?"

He began:	*Harvest is in,*
Robbie said:	*Winter begins,*
Archie added:	*Witches are about!*
Malcolm:	*Strange shadows,*
Robbie:	*Story and songs,*
Archie:	*Witching Halloween*
Malcolm:	*Haunted Halloween*
Robbie:	*Ghostly Halloween is here!*

Granny said, "Bonny! All you need's a tune. My pa was the best fiddler on this mountain." She looked at the boys. "Ary one of you know how to fiddle?"

"No," Robbie said, "but I'm pretty good with a comb if you have a bit of thin paper."

Malcolm brought Robbie a comb wrapped in tissue paper from a shoe box. Robbie pressed it to his mouth and tested for sound. At first the crisp paper tickled and shivered his lips. Then he got the hang of it. A humming tune began to come.

"All right," Robbie said. "What'll we sing?"

"You know 'Gentle Annie'?" Malcolm asked. "Granny loves that song."

Robbie hummed into the comb. As usual the music stirred in him gladness and sadness, at the same time. He liked to play. Everyone said that he could make a comb talk or laugh or cry, all right.

They sang "Gentle Annie" and went on to "Arkansas Traveler." They were all tapping

their feet and clapping their hands when the song ended.

After they caught their breath, Malcolm said, "Your clothes are dry now. I'll lead you to a path I know. You can follow it to the road, where you'll know your way home."

Robbie knew they must leave while the moon was still high to give them light, but he had a queasy feeling about going into the strange woods again.

"What about Daisy?" he asked.

"If she's in our hollow," Malcolm said, "I'll find her in the morning and bring her home."

Archie said, "Maybe we better wait here until morning and save you the trouble."

"No trouble," Malcolm said.

Robbie looked at Archie. They couldn't put off any longer going back into the night.

"Don't be afeared," Granny Duncan said. "Once you start, fear grows and grows. You hear the rustle of a leaf and think it's a bear. A hooty owl cries, and you feel eyes all about you

— and somethin' behind your back grabbin' at you. I know."

She nodded her white head up and down. "After what happened to my boys, I was afeared. Dinna trust nobody on my place, from that day to this, but now I want friends for my lad."

Robbie and Archie went into the cookroom and put on their dry clothes. When they returned, Granny went to the door with the three boys.

"Thank you very much," Robbie said to her. "I'll never forget our Highland Halloween party."

"It was better than going to the party at the school," Archie agreed. "Except for the ghost."

"Ghost?" Malcolm asked.

"We saw something white coming at us from behind the barn," Robbie told him. "At least we thought —"

"We *saw* it," Archie declared. "Remember, I was in front."

"They say sperits do walk on Halloween night," Granny said, "but I niver saw a ghost on my place, niver."

Malcolm opened the door. The boys followed him into the misty moonlight. Robbie turned and called to Granny, who stood in the lighted doorway, "Good-by."

"By-eye-ee-eye-ee-eye-eee!" echoed the peaks behind the barn.

Then the ghost came. Large and white, it appeared in the mist and moved through the barnyard directly toward the boys.

Robbie couldn't move. He felt Archie clutch his elbow. He saw that Malcolm had stopped, too, staring in surprise. They had all seen it. The ghost was real and not his imagination.

The white figure loomed larger and larger as it came nearer. Robbie began to tremble. Prickles ran along his arm and his hair felt as if it were standing straight up on his head. The ghost was almost upon them now.

Then Granny cried, "My sheets. My white sheets are gone from the clothesline."

Malcolm laughed and Robbie grinned. They saw the ghost's four legs now. They saw its brindled sides. They heard the ghost's low "Mo-ooo." The ghost was Daisy. She must have run into Granny's sheets and tangled them on her horns. Then she couldn't get the sheets off.

"So-o-oo, Bossy," Robbie called soothingly.

Daisy lowed and came to him. The boys lifted the sheets from her horns and patted her head. "So-o-o, Daisy, you're all right," Robbie said. "We're going home now."

Malcolm brought a rope from the house. Robbie knotted it around Daisy's neck. She followed the boys eagerly as if she were glad to be found.

Malcolm led the way through the dark shadows of the woods as easily as if it had been daylight. He seemed to enjoy walking at night.

The night *is* beautiful, Robbie thought, and

all the things Archie and I were afraid of turned out to be harmless.

Halfway up the slope, Malcolm stopped and pointed under the shadow of a cliff. "There's a fox lair there," he said. "I found it last spring when the mother fox was away, and I played with the little foxes. I'll show you next year."

Finally he came to a narrow path. "This deer crossing leads to the road," he said. "Then turn right. Follow it into town."

"Good-by, Malcolm, see you at school," Robbie called as he led Daisy down the deer path after Archie.

The moon was so pretty and the air smelled so clean and sweet that Robbie felt like singing. A tune came into his head. He hummed a minute, then sang:

"Daisy-cow has run away! What'll I do-do-do?"

Archie called back, "That pesky cow's become a ghost. Boo-hoo-hoo!"

The boys laughed and went on singing new

lines. Daisy plodded behind them as if she were used to having a ballad made, and sung, in her honor.